Here's what kids and g

say about the Magic Tr

"Oh, man . . . the Magic Tree House series is really exciting!"

—Christina

"I like the Magic Tree House series. I stay up all night reading them. Even on school nights!"

—Peter

"Jack and Annie have opened a door to a world of literacy that I know will continue throughout the lives of my students."

—Deborah H.

"As a librarian, I have seen many happy young readers coming into the library to check out the next Magic Tree House book in the series."

—Lynne H.

Magic Tree House® Merlin Missions

#1: Christmas in Camelot
#2: Haunted Castle on Hallows Eve
#3: Summer of the Sea Serpent
#4: Winter of the Ice Wizard
#5: Carnival at Candlelight
#6: Season of the Sandstorms
#7: Night of the New Magicians
#8: Blizzard of the Blue Moon
#9: Dragon of the Red Dawn
#10: Monday with a Mad Genius
#11: Dark Day in the Deep Sea
#12: Eve of the Emperor Penguin
#13: Moonlight on the Magic Flute
#14: A Good Night for Ghosts
#15: Leprechaun in Late Winter
#16: A Ghost Tale for Christmas Time
#17: A Crazy Day with Cobras
#18: Dogs in the Dead of Night
#19: Abe Lincoln at Last!
#20: A Perfect Time for Pandas
#21: Stallion by Starlight
#22: Hurry Up, Houdini!
#23: High Time for Heroes
#24: Soccer on Sunday
#25: Shadow of the Shark
#26: Balto of the Blue Dawn
#27: Night of the Ninth Dragon

For a list of all the Magic Tree House® titles,
visit MagicTreeHouse.com.

MAGIC TREE HOUSE®

MERLIN MISSIONS

#14 A GOOD NIGHT FOR GHOSTS

BY MARY POPE OSBORNE

ILLUSTRATED BY SAL MURDOCCA

A STEPPING STONE BOOK™

Random House New York

This is a work of fiction. All incidents and dialogue, and all characters with the exception of some well-known historical and public figures, are products of the author's imagination and are not to be construed as real. Where real-life historical or public figures appear, the situations, incidents, and dialogues concerning those persons are fictional and are not intended to depict actual events or to change the fictional nature of the work. In all other respects, any resemblance to persons living or dead is entirely coincidental.

 Published in the United States by Random House Children's Books, a division of Penguin Random House LLC, New York. Originally published in hardcover as Magic Tree House #42 in 2009.

Visit us on the Web!
SteppingStonesBooks.com
MagicTreeHouse.com
randomhousekids.com

Educators and librarians, for a variety of teaching tools, visit us at
RHTeachersLibrarians.com

The Library of Congress has cataloged the hardcover edition of this work as follows:
Osborne, Mary Pope.
A good night for ghosts / by Mary Pope Osborne ; illustrated by Sal Murdocca.
p. cm. — (Magic tree house ; #42)
"A Merlin mission."
"A Stepping Stone book."
Summary: Jack and Annie must travel back in time to New Orleans in 1915 to help a teenaged Louis Armstrong fulfill his destiny and become the "King of Jazz."
ISBN 978-0-375-85648-8 (trade) — ISBN 978-0-375-95648-5 (lib. bdg.) —
ISBN 978-0-375-89464-0 (ebook) — ISBN 978-0-375-85649-5 (pbk.)
[1. Time travel—Fiction. 2. Magic—Fiction. 3. Armstrong, Louis, 1901–1971—Childhood and youth—Fiction. 4. Jazz—Fiction. 5. African Americans—Fiction. 6. Brothers and sisters—Fiction. 7. New Orleans (La.)—History—20th century—Fiction.]
I. Murdocca, Sal, ill. II. Title.
PZ7.O81167Gon2009 [Fic]—dc22 2008042061

Printed in the United States of America
23

This book has been officially leveled by using the F&P Text Level Gradient™ Leveling System.

Random House Children's Books supports the First Amendment and celebrates the right to read.

For Will, who always wanted
me to write this book

Dear Reader,

Years ago, my husband, Will, and I lived for several weeks in the French Quarter in New Orleans while Will was performing in a play at the Saenger Theatre. During that time we fell in love with the city's architecture, food, and especially its music. Every night after Will's show, we sought out our favorite jazz bands. One of our best memories is visiting the New Orleans Jazz Museum and seeing the first cornet played by a young Louis Armstrong, who grew up to be one of the greatest jazz performers the world has ever known. Soon after that stay in New Orleans, we started collecting Louis Armstrong's early recordings and began learning about his life.

I always knew it was only a matter of time before Jack, Annie, and I would have an adventure in New Orleans with Louis Armstrong. And now I can say it was one of the best adventures we've ever had.

Mary Pope Osborne

CONTENTS

"I was so happy I did not know what to do. I had hit the big time. I was up North [playing] with the greats. . . . My boyhood dream had come true at last."

—Louis Armstrong,

from *Satchmo: My Life in New Orleans*

Prologue

One summer day in Frog Creek, Pennsylvania, a mysterious tree house appeared in the woods. A brother and sister named Jack and Annie soon learned that the tree house was magic—it could take them to any time and any place in history. They also learned that the tree house belonged to Morgan le Fay, a magical librarian from the legendary realm of Camelot.

After Jack and Annie had traveled on many adventures for Morgan, Merlin the magician began sending them on "Merlin Missions" in the tree house. With help from two young sorcerers named Teddy and Kathleen, Jack and Annie visited four *mythical* places and found valuable objects to help save Camelot.

On their next four Merlin Missions, Jack and Annie once again traveled to *real* times and *real* places in history. After they proved to Merlin that they knew how to use magic wisely, he awarded them the Wand of Dianthus, a powerful magic wand that helped them make their own magic. With the help of the wand, Jack and Annie were able to find four secrets of happiness to help Merlin when he was in trouble.

Now Merlin wants Jack and Annie to bring happiness to others—by helping four creative people give their special gifts to the world. . . .

CHAPTER ONE

Way Down Yonder in New Orleans

Jack was asleep. He was dreaming that he was sleeping on a boat. It was rocking back and forth, back and forth. . . .

"Jack."

Jack opened his eyes. It was just getting light outside. Rain was tapping against the windowpane. *Tappity-tap-tap.* Jack closed his eyes again.

"Jack, get up."

Jack opened one eye and looked up. Annie stood next to his bed. She was already dressed.

She was even wearing her raincoat. "They're here," she whispered.

"No, they're not," Jack said. He closed his eye.

"Yes, they are," said Annie. "They're waiting for us."

"How do you know?" Jack asked.

"I dreamed it," said Annie.

"Oh, you dreamed it." Jack turned over and pulled the covers over his head. "Go back to bed. It's really early, and it's raining."

"Come on, Jack," said Annie. "I saw them. They were wearing their cloaks and looking out the tree house window."

"Great," said Jack. "I just dreamed I was sleeping on a boat."

"But *my* dream was real, Jack," said Annie.

Jack pretended to snore.

"Okay," said Annie. "I guess you want me to go there all by myself. You want me to have a great adventure while you just lie here, dreaming about sleeping. If that's really what you want, I'll leave you alone."

"Good," said Jack. "Have fun."

"Don't worry, I will," said Annie, and she left Jack's room.

Jack lay still for a moment, listening to the rain fall outside. *Darn,* he thought, *what if she's right?*

Jack heaved a sigh. Then he climbed out of bed. He pulled on his clothes and grabbed his backpack. He slipped down the stairs, put on his rain boots and raincoat, then headed out the front door.

Annie was standing on the porch, waiting for him. "Ready?" she said.

Jack just grunted. But as he and Annie took off into the cool, rainy dawn, he woke up completely. As they charged up the sidewalk, Jack's heart pounded with excitement. By the time they headed into the Frog Creek woods, Jack felt like he'd dreamed Annie's dream, too.

Raindrops tapped on tree branches. Jack and Annie scrunched over fallen red and gold leaves until they came to the tallest oak. Jack looked up.

"Ta-da!" said Annie.

The tree house *was* back. And Teddy and

Kathleen were dressed in their dark cloaks, looking out the window.

"Good morning!" called Kathleen.

"We dreamed about you!" said Jack. "At least Annie did."

Teddy and Kathleen smiled, as if this news didn't surprise them at all.

Annie and Jack started up the rope ladder. When they climbed inside the tree house, they hugged the two young enchanters. "Welcome," said Kathleen. Her beautiful sea-blue eyes sparkled.

"Do you have a new mission for us?" said Jack.

"Indeed," said Teddy, smiling. "Just like last time, Merlin wants you to help a creative person bring his gifts to the world."

"And *this* will help you," said Kathleen. She pulled a book from her cloak.

"Great!" said Jack. He took the book from Kathleen. The cover showed a street parade with musicians playing trumpets and trombones. The title was *A History of New Orleans Music.*

"New Orleans?" said Annie.

"Yes, New Orleans, Louisiana," said Kathleen.

"You will love this city," said Teddy.

"Cool," said Annie.

"And here is your magic flute." Kathleen picked up a gleaming silver flute from the corner of the tree house. It was the magic flute Jack had played on their adventure in Vienna, Austria. "Only this time . . ." Kathleen tossed the flute into the air. It hovered for a moment, then began to twirl around and around. There was a flash of blue light—and the flute was gone! Floating in its place was a shining brass instrument.

Kathleen plucked the instrument from the air. "This time you will play a magic trumpet," she said.

"Oh, man," breathed Jack. "That's incredible."

"Yeah," said Annie. "I've always wanted to play the trumpet."

Kathleen laughed. "Well, this is your chance," she said. "The trumpet's magic will make you a brilliant performer."

"But the magic can only happen once," Teddy reminded Jack and Annie, "just as on your last journey with the magic flute. Play the trumpet only when you face your greatest danger."

"And while one of us plays, the other has to make up a song, right?" said Annie. "And whatever we sing will come true."

"Precisely," said Teddy.

"Um . . . what danger will we face in New Orleans?" asked Jack.

"Perhaps none," said Teddy. "But keep the magic trumpet with you just in case. And remember, after you have played it, the magic will be gone and it will become an ordinary trumpet."

"Got it," said Jack. He took a deep breath.

"Okay," said Annie. "Ready?"

"Wait," said Jack. "Can you tell us what kind of creative genius we're looking for?"

"We can do more than that," said Kathleen with a smile. "We can tell you his name. It is Louis Armstrong."

"Louis Armstrong," repeated Jack. He knew that name.

"He is the King of Jazz," said Teddy.

"The King of Jazz?" said Annie. "Cool!"

"Yes," said Kathleen. "But Louis Armstrong won't know that when you meet him. It is your job to put him on the right path."

"To give his gifts to the world," said Annie. "Got it."

"Good," said Teddy. "And now you should go."

"Right," said Jack. He pointed at the cover of the book. "I wish we could go there," he said. "To New Orleans!"

"To meet the King of Jazz!" said Annie.

"Good luck!" said Teddy as he and Kathleen waved good-bye.

The wind started to blow.

The tree house started to spin.

It spun faster and faster.

Then everything was still.

Absolutely still.

CHAPTER TWO

Money Blues

The hot, muggy air was filled with noise. Jack and Annie heard the *clippity-clop* of horses' hooves. They heard voices calling out "Crawfish pies!" "Buttermilk!" "Gumbo for sale here!"

Jack looked down at his and Annie's clothes. They were both wearing white shirts and dark trousers with suspenders. Jack's backpack had turned into a cloth bag. Neither Jack nor Annie was wearing shoes.

"Wow, we're barefoot. That's cool," said Annie. "And at least I can run in these pants. I like them a lot better than the dress I wore on our last mission."

"Yeah." Jack smiled, remembering Annie's long, frilly dress in Vienna and his velvet coat and white wig. "I like being barefoot, too," he said. "But what year did we come to? I can't tell from our outfits."

Jack and Annie looked out the window. The tree house had landed in a grove of palm trees. Not far away, steamboats churned down a river. Below them was a bustling city scene. Rows of stores lined both sides of a wide street. Vendors were selling food from carts. Women shoppers wore long skirts, and men wore white suits and hats.

Mule carts and horse-drawn buggies bumped alongside a few antique-looking cars. Moving down the middle of the street were red and green train cars. Each one was attached to an electric line overhead.

"This is definitely a long time ago," said Jack. "But when exactly?"

"I can't tell," said Annie.

"Maybe our research book can help us," said Jack. "I'll look up Louis Armstrong." Jack looked in the index of *A History of New Orleans Music* and found a chapter on Louis Armstrong. He read:

Born in New Orleans in 1901, Louis Armstrong grew up to be one of the greatest jazz musicians who ever lived.

A photo showed an African American man playing a trumpet. His cheeks were puffed out and his eyes were closed. Stage lights were shining on him. Thousands of people were in the audience. The caption under the photo read *Louis Armstrong, King of Jazz.*

"So what is *jazz* exactly?" asked Annie.

"It's a kind of music," said Jack.

"Well, yeah, but what kind?" said Annie.

Jack looked up *jazz* in the glossary of their book. He read:

Jazz began in New Orleans in the early 1900s and was first played by African

Americans. It is a style of music that has a strong beat and is played with lots of feeling. Jazz melodies are often made up on the spot.

"Got it," said Annie. "Read more about Louis."

Jack flipped back to the pages about Louis Armstrong and read:

As a young teenager, Louis Armstrong often performed with "kid bands" on the streets of the city. Eventually he played with older musicians in dance halls and developed his musical talents performing on Mississippi riverboats. When he was twenty-one, he moved to Chicago, where—

"Stop. That's all we need," Annie broke in.

"It is?" asked Jack.

"Yep, we'll just ask someone what the date is," said Annie. "Then we can figure out how old Louis Armstrong is, and we'll know where to look for him: the streets, a dance hall, or on the Mississippi River."

Annie picked up the magic trumpet. She tucked

it under her arm and started down the rope ladder.

"I *guess* that's a plan," murmured Jack. "Sort of." He put the New Orleans book in his bag and followed her.

In their bare feet, Jack and Annie hurried a short distance to the wide, busy street. A sign read CANAL STREET.

The sidewalks on both sides of Canal Street were crowded with vendors pushing carts and shouting in rich, loud voices.

"Buttermilk! Buttermilk! Fresh from the buttermilk man! Bring out your bucket! Bring out your can!" shouted a man.

"Blackberries! Mighty fine! Three sacks for a dime!" called an old woman.

"Read all the news! Chase away the blues!" sang a boy with newspapers.

"Let's buy a paper," said Jack. "It'll tell us the date."

Jack and Annie ran over to the boy selling newspapers.

"A paper, please," said Annie.

"A penny, please," said the boy.

Jack and Annie dug into their pockets.

"Uh-oh," said Annie. "No money."

"Uh-oh," said the boy. "No paper." He started to walk away.

"Wait, please," said Jack. "Can you just tell us the date?"

"October thirty-first, the eve of All Saints' Day," said the boy. "You didn't know that?"

"Uh, not really," said Jack.

"And what year is it?" Annie asked.

The newsboy scowled. "It's 1915! Don't you two know anything? Who are you?"

Before Jack could think of an answer, Annie blurted out, "We're musicians. We came all the way from Frog Creek, Pennsylvania." She held up their trumpet.

"Oh, right. And it's a different year in Frog Creek, Pennsylvania, than here in New Orleans, Louisiana! I forgot!" The newsboy headed up the street, laughing at his own joke.

"Well, *yeah*," said Annie.

Jack laughed. "Okay, Louis Armstrong was born in 1901, so if it's 1915 . . ."

"He's fourteen years old," said Annie. "So that means he's playing with kid bands in the streets. Excuse me!" she called to the buttermilk man. "Can you tell us where some kid bands might be playing today?"

"Try Jackson Square in the French Quarter," said the man.

"What's the French Quarter?" asked Jack.

"It's the oldest section of the city," said the buttermilk man. "Catch that streetcar that's stopping up ahead! It will take you right there."

"Thanks!" said Annie. She and Jack ran up the sidewalk.

"So I guess those train cars in the street are called streetcars," said Jack.

"Makes sense!" said Annie.

Jack and Annie ran to a streetcar stop. They

stood in line and then climbed aboard. "Oh, wait," Jack said to Annie. "We can't! We don't have money!" He started to leave.

"Hey, sonny, are you coming or going?" said the conductor.

"Sorry. We made a mistake," said Jack. "We don't have any money."

"Don't worry, there's no fare today. It's the eve of All Saints' Day," said the conductor.

"Oh! Good," said Jack. He and Annie chose a wooden seat near the door and sat down.

"Could you tell us when to get out for Jackson Square in the French Quarter?" Annie asked the conductor.

"Sure thing," the conductor said.

Annie rested their magic trumpet on her lap. "Lucky for us we came here on the eve of All Saints' Day," she said to Jack.

"Yeah, but what does that mean?" said Jack. As the streetcar headed along Canal, he looked up All Saints' Day in their book. He read aloud:

November first is celebrated as All Saints' Day in New Orleans. It is a day to honor those who have passed away. Sometimes on the eve of All Saints' Day, people wear costumes and have parties and parades. Considered the spookiest night of the year, the eve of All Saints' Day is a good time for ghost sightings.

"The eve of All Saints' Day sounds like Halloween," said Annie. "It's the same day, too: October thirty-first."

"Yeah," said Jack. "But what do they mean, 'a good time for ghost sightings'?" He kept reading:

The city of New Orleans is often called the most haunted city in America. According to legend, the old blacksmith shop on Bourbon Street is haunted by the ghost of the famous pirate Jean Lafitte. Some say that Saint Louis Cathedral is haunted by a Spanish priest, and that a hotel on Chartres Street is haunted by Confederate

soldiers. There have been ghost sightings in many other places throughout the city as well.

"Ooh, sounds scary," said Annie.

"Huh," said Jack. "Well!" He slammed the book shut. "Forget ghosts. We didn't come to New Orleans to look for ghosts. We came here to look for Louis Armstrong, the King of Jazz."

CHAPTER THREE

Coal Cart Blues

The streetcar turned onto a crowded, busy street. Lively music blared from restaurants and dance halls.

"We're in the French Quarter now, and you're the next stop," the conductor said to Jack and Annie. "Head down St. Peter Street toward the Mississippi River. You'll run right into Jackson Square."

"Thanks!" Jack put the research book back in his bag. Annie tucked the trumpet under her arm. When the streetcar came to a stop, they hopped off.

"Good luck playing that horn, missy!" said the conductor.

"Thanks, I'll need it!" said Annie.

As the streetcar pulled away, Jack and Annie looked around. "Hey, this is Bourbon Street," said Annie, pointing to a street sign. "Isn't that the street with the haunted blacksmith shop?"

"Don't think about that," said Jack. "Let's head down St. Peter."

Jack and Annie left Bourbon Street and started down St. Peter Street. They passed tall, narrow houses painted pale green, yellow, and pink. Vines grew up walls and twined around iron balconies. Alleys led to courtyards with trickling fountains.

"I like the buildings in New Orleans," said Annie.

"Yeah, and it smells good, too," said Jack.

Delicious food smells filled the air. From a mule-drawn cart, an old woman cried out, "Waffles! Get your waffles here! Yes sir, fresh, hot waffles!"

Jack was getting hungry. Outside a restaurant was a sign that read:

Special! Dinner 10 cents.

"Gosh, things are cheap in 1915," said Jack. "Too bad we don't even have a dime."

"Yeah," said Annie. "Oh, look!" She pointed to a grand cathedral with soaring spires. "A cathedral! That must be the place with the ghost of the Spanish priest."

"Why do you like ghosts so much?" said Jack.

"I don't like ghosts so much," said Annie.

"Well, you keep talking about them," said Jack.

"I'm just pointing things out," said Annie. "You're the one who brought up ghosts in the first place."

"Well, let's forget them," said Jack. He didn't like ghosts. He didn't even like thinking about them.

Soon Jack and Annie came to a huge green park with an iron fence around it. A sign at the entrance read: JACKSON SQUARE.

"We found it!" said Jack.

Outside the iron fence, in the hot afternoon sunlight, small bands of barefoot kids were playing music. Some strummed banjos. Others played harmonicas or long tin horns. Three boys sang in harmony. A couple of the smallest kids passed around hats, collecting money for the different bands.

"Where's Louis Armstrong?" Annie asked Jack. "No one here looks like the picture in our book."

"Of course not," said Jack. "The picture shows him as a grown-up. He wouldn't look the same when he's fourteen."

"I'll ask," said Annie. She went up to a small girl passing a hat. "Excuse me, is there a musician here named Louis Armstrong?"

"Louis Armstrong? You mean Dipper?" asked the girl.

"I guess . . . ," said Annie.

"Hey, Little Mack!" the girl shouted to the biggest kid in the singing trio. "Where's Dipper Armstrong?"

"Just saw him—he's at the River Café!" shouted Little Mack.

"Where's that?" Annie asked.

"Down by the river," said the small girl. She pointed beyond the square. "Walk down Decatur Street and you'll see it." The girl held up the hat, as if asking for a donation.

"Sorry, no money," said Jack.

"But thanks for your help," said Annie. She and Jack left the square. They hurried along Decatur Street.

"So Dipper must be a nickname for Louis Armstrong," said Jack.

"Yeah," said Annie. "And Dipper must be playing music at the café."

"There it is," said Jack. He pointed to a red sign on a slanted rooftop.

"Doughnuts, yum," said Annie.

Jack and Annie walked under a striped red awning. Waiters in white jackets were running around with trays of coffee and delicious-smelling doughnuts. Jack's mouth watered.

"That's funny. There's no music here," said Annie. "Excuse us," she called to one of the waiters. "Have you seen Louis Armstrong? Or Dip—"

"Did you come here to buy something, kids?" the waiter interrupted rudely.

"No, we don't have any money—" started Jack.

"Then out, boy!" the waiter shouted. "No begging in here!"

"He's not begging!" said Annie. "We're looking for—"

"I know beggars when I see them! Out!" said the waiter.

"Let's go. I don't think Dipper's in here, anyway," said Jack.

"Wait a minute, I have to tell them that we're not beggars!" Annie said.

"It's not worth it, come on," said Jack.

Jack was mad, too, but he pulled Annie out from under the awning. "I think it's the way we look," he said. "Our clothes make us look poor. And we don't have shoes on."

"It's not fair," said Annie.

"Forget it. We'll ask someone else where to find Dipper," said Jack.

On the street by the café was a mule cart filled with coal. A young teenager was putting a bucket and shovel into the back of the cart. He was barefoot and wore clothes like Jack's and Annie's.

"Excuse me!" Jack called. "Do you know Louis Armstrong? Or Dipper?"

The boy turned. When he saw Jack and Annie, he grinned. He had the friendliest smile Jack had ever seen. "Louis Armstrong?" he said. "That's me. How can I help you, man?"

Jack was at a loss for words. He hadn't thought about what to say to Louis Armstrong when they found him.

"Hi, Dipper!" said Annie, walking up to the boy. "We're Jack and Annie from Frog Creek, Pennsylvania. Friends of ours told us to find you when we came to New Orleans."

"What friends?" asked Dipper.

"Teddy and Kathleen," said Annie.

The boy looked puzzled. But then his gaze fell on Annie's trumpet. "Hey, nice horn. Can you play that thing?"

"Only when the time is right," said Annie.

"And when's that?" asked Dipper.

"I won't know till I feel it," said Annie.

Dipper smiled his radiant smile again. "Ha! I know just what you mean!" he said. He wiped his hand on his pants and held it out to shake. "Any friends of Teddy and Kathleen's are friends of mine."

As Jack shook Dipper's hand, he sputtered, "You—you know Teddy and Kathleen?"

"No, man, never heard of them," said Dipper. "But I consider everybody my friend."

"Oh. Oh!" said Annie. She and Jack laughed.

"Only problem is I can't hang out with y'all right now," said Dipper. He climbed onto the mule cart.

"Where—where you going, man?" asked Jack.

"I'm making my rounds with this coal cart," said Dipper. "And I have lots more work to do today. But be sure to look me up the next time you come to town. And say hi to my pals, Teddy and Kathleen." Dipper waved at them and then shook the reins. "Go 'long, mule," he said.

The mule clopped over the brick street, pulling the coal cart away from the River Café.

Louis Armstrong was gone.

CHAPTER FOUR

Potato Head Blues

"What now?" Jack said.

"We have to follow him," said Annie. "We can't let him out of our sight."

Jack and Annie walked quickly after the mule cart. The hot brick road burned their feet. "Ow, ow, ow," they both whispered.

"So let's figure out—ow—what we're going to say to him," said Jack.

"Simple," said Annie. "We'll tell him we'd like to work with him. And then while we're working, we'll start talking to him about music. And put him on the right path to becoming the King of Jazz."

"Hmm," said Jack. It wasn't much of a plan, but he couldn't think of anything better.

Up ahead, Dipper's mule cart stopped near the back of a candy shop.

"Hey, Dipper!" yelled Annie.

Dipper looked over his shoulder. He smiled. "What's going on? Y'all are sticking to me like glue," he said.

"Well, actually, we were wondering—" started Jack.

"If we could work with you?" finished Annie.

"Work with me?" said Dipper. "I'm just delivering coal."

"Yeah, we know. We think it might be fun," said Annie.

Dipper laughed. "Y'all are crazy," he said.

"No, we're not. We just like to work," said Annie.

"Yeah, yeah, we really do," said Jack.

Dipper laughed again. "Okay. I reckon there's

enough work to go around today," he said. "There's extra shovels and buckets in the cart."

"Cool. Just tell us what to do, Dipper," said Annie.

"Fill your buckets with coal and toss each bucket load into the bin," said Dipper. He pointed to a large wooden box at the back of the small candy shop. "Twelve bucket loads should do it."

"Got it," said Annie.

Annie carefully set the magic trumpet on the ground near Dipper's cart. Jack left his cloth bag beside it. Dipper handed each of them a heavy shovel and a tin bucket from the back of the cart. Then all three of them started shoveling coal.

Dipper whistled and worked quickly. But Jack and Annie had a hard time handling their heavy shovels. Whenever the shovels tipped to the side, all the coal fell off. Finally they both just grabbed pieces of coal with their hands and tossed them into their buckets.

The afternoon sun beat down on Jack's back as

he worked. He was sweaty and short of breath. His hands were black from picking up the coal, and his clothes were covered with coal dust. *This is a terrible job*, he thought. He wondered how Dipper could be so cheerful.

"So, Dipper," said Annie, "do you like music?"

Dipper's answer was drowned out as he dumped a load of coal into the bin.

"What'd you say?" Jack called to Dipper.

Dipper answered again, but Jack didn't hear him because a buggy rumbled by. *This is a bad time for a serious discussion*, Jack thought. He could hardly think in the burning sun.

As Dipper shoveled more coal, he started singing a song that seemed to give words to how Jack felt:

I've got those coal cart blues.
I'm really all confused—
I'm about to lose my very mind.

But Dipper didn't seem confused at all, or

about to lose his mind. He had a warm, raspy voice, and his song had a lively beat.

"Dipper! Dipper! Dipper!" some kids called.

Dipper stopped singing. Three boys were running toward the coal cart. They were the singing trio Jack and Annie had seen on Jackson Square.

"I know you're working," said one of the kids. "But quit early today, Dipper! We just got a gig to sing in the parade."

"Sorry, can't do it, Little Mack," said Dipper.

Little Mack wasn't exactly little, Jack noticed. He looked like he weighed over two hundred pounds.

"Come on, Dipper," said another boy.

"Gotta work, Happy," said Dipper.

"Aww, Dipper," said Happy. He didn't look happy at all.

"Come on, Dipper!" said the third boy.

"Can't do it, Big Nose," said Dipper.

Jack looked at Big Nose's nose. It was really quite small.

"Aww," said Happy again.

"Go on now. Y'all sound just fine by yourselves," said Dipper. "Go on to the parade and have fun."

"But—" Big Nose began.

"Listen," said Dipper. "Since sunup, I've delivered five cartloads of coal. I get paid fifteen cents a load. That makes seventy-five cents I'm going to take home to my family tonight. How much did you fellas make on the square today? How much you going to make in the parade?"

The three boys were silent.

"I've got a steady job now," said Dipper. "You don't need me. Go on to the parade and have a good time."

The three boys stared at Dipper for a long moment. "Come on, fellas," Little Mack said finally. "Let him be. Ever since he got back from the Waif's Home, he's turned into a mama's boy."

Jack wondered what the Waif's Home was.

Dipper watched the three boys walk off. Then he looked at Jack and Annie. "Little Mack, Happy, and Big Nose Sidney are old buddies of mine," he explained with a sigh. "We used to have a quartet. We sang everywhere together."

"Dipper, can't you take just a *little* time off and go with your buddies to sing in the parade?" asked Annie.

"Nope," said Dipper. "That's just the way it has to be."

Dipper went back to shoveling coal. Jack wanted to ask him about the Waif's Home, but Dipper didn't look like he wanted to talk. He didn't sing anymore as he filled up his coal bucket.

If Dipper doesn't perform, he'll never grow up to be the King of Jazz, Jack thought. *He'll never give his gifts to the world.*

Finally Annie broke the silence. "Dipper, do you have to support your family all by yourself? You're pretty young for that, aren't you?"

"I'm not young. I'm fourteen," said Dipper. "Mama Lucy, Mayann, and baby Clarence are all depending on me."

"Is that your family?" asked Jack.

"Yep, and I love them a lot," said Dipper.

"I understand," said Annie.

"Me too," said Jack. "But what about giving your gifts to the world?"

Dipper laughed. "I can't afford gifts for Lady the mule. How am I going to afford gifts for the *world*?"

"What about your *musical* gifts?" asked Jack.

"Okay, good idea. I'll sing a song to Lady on her birthday," he said. "Let's go now."

Dipper tossed his shovel into the bucket. Then he reached into his pocket and took out some change. "Tomorrow I'll be getting paid fifteen cents for this load," he said. "In case I don't see you again, here's your share: five cents for you and five for you."

"No, no, keep it," said Annie. "You should keep it all for your family, Dipper."

"What? That's not right," said Dipper.

"It *is* right," said Jack.

"Then what did y'all do that work for?" asked Dipper.

"We didn't do that much," Jack said. "Not nearly as much as you did. It was a lot harder job than I thought it would be."

"Then why did y'all keep working?" asked Dipper.

"It was fun hanging out with you," said Annie.

Dipper laughed. "Well, you two sure are a couple of potato heads," he said.

"What's that mean?" asked Annie.

"It means you don't have any more brains than a pair of potatoes," said Dipper.

Jack and Annie just laughed.

"Sure you won't take any money?" said Dipper.

"Absolutely!" said Annie.

"Well, thanks a million for your help," said Dipper. He climbed back into the driver's seat of the cart. "Hey, want me and Lady to give y'all a ride back to the coal yard?"

"Yes!" said Jack and Annie together.

"Good. Climb on!" said Dipper.

"Thanks, man!" said Jack.

Annie grabbed their trumpet. Jack grabbed his bag, and they sat on the cart bench next to Dipper. Jack was still hot and sweaty. He was tired and his arms were sore. But for some reason, he felt great.

"Let's go, Lady," said Dipper.

Lady the mule began pulling the creaky cart along the Mississippi River. And Dipper began singing again:

I've got those coal cart blues.
I'm really all confused. . . .

CHAPTER FIVE

Go 'Long, Mule

The sky had grown cloudy, and a warm breeze was blowing.

Dipper stopped the cart and listened. "Hear that?" he said. "Parade's coming this way."

Jack heard band music in the distance.

"Is that parade for All Saints' Day?" asked Annie.

"Maybe. Or maybe for a million other things," said Dipper. "Folks in this city will find any excuse for a parade."

Soon the parade came into view.

Horseback riders wore plumed hats and black masks. Following them were people dressed up as clowns, kings, queens, fairies with fluttering wings, ghosts, and skeletons.

"We read that New Orleans might be the most haunted city in the country," Annie said to Dipper, "especially on the eve of All Saints' Day. We heard there're *real* ghosts in a cathedral, a hotel, and a blacksmith shop."

"Yeah, and plenty more places, too," said Dipper. "But I'm not afraid of ghosts. I'm not afraid of anything."

"Me neither!" said Annie.

"Um, me neither," said Jack.

A band followed the people in costumes. The musicians were playing trumpets, tubas, trombones, and drums—lots of drums. The joyous music filled the New Orleans air. Jack and Annie couldn't help nodding their heads in time to the beat. Jack noticed that Dipper was nodding his head, too.

"Hey, there're the fellas!" said Annie.

Happy, Little Mack, and Big Nose Sidney were walking alongside the band, singing their hearts out.

"Looks like they're having fun!" said Annie. She nudged Jack. "Doesn't it?"

"Yeah!" said Jack. "A lot of fun! Music is so much fun! I wish I had musical talent! You're so lucky, Dipper!"

"You really are, Dipper!" said Annie. "Musical talent is really a great gift to share with the world!"

Dipper just shook his head, as if he thought they were crazy. "Biggest potato heads I've ever met," he said.

Jack and Annie laughed.

Dipper gave the reins a shake. "Go 'long, Lady. Keep me on my path."

How weird that Dipper said that, Jack thought. Their mission was to keep him on the right path, too—the path to becoming the King of Jazz.

As Lady plodded along the bank of the

Mississippi, Dipper started singing nonsense words:

Skid-dat-de-dat
Skid-dat-de-doo!

"That sounds so cool," said Jack. "What's that song?"

"Not a song. I'm just scat-singing, man," said Dipper.

"Scat-singing?" said Annie. "What's that?"

"When you can't think of words, just sing sounds," said Dipper. "Make 'em up. If you put your heart in it, folks will understand you."

"I didn't know a person could make music like that," said Jack.

"Heck, yeah, you can make music any way you want," said Dipper. "Just listen to the world: There's church bells, the washerwoman singing about her wash, the ragman blasting his tin horn for folks to bring out their rags. Folks selling things, like that pie man. Listen to him."

Dipper pointed to a man sitting in a red wagon, calling out in a strong, rich voice, "Sweet potato! Sweet potato pie! Lemon pie! Apple pie! Any pie you like!"

"Listen to that voice," said Dipper. "That's music. And listen to those sounds—" Dipper pointed to some women walking beside the road.

The women carried baskets on their heads and called out in singsong voices, "Blue-berries!" "Rasp-berries!" "Black-berrieeeeeeeeeeeeeeees!"

"I see what you mean," said Annie. "Music is everywhere."

"You got it, girl," said Dipper. "You can even hear it in Lady's hoofbeats. Listen."

Jack listened to the rhythmic *clippity-clop, clippity-clop* of the mule.

"See? There you go!" said Dipper. "That's a song—*Go 'long, mule, go 'long, mule.*"

Jack and Annie listened to the steady music of Lady's hoofbeats, until finally the mule came to a stop.

"Well, here we are at the coal yard," said Dipper. "I'll leave Lady here till tomorrow."

They all jumped to the ground.

"Thanks for your music, Lady." Dipper patted the mule on her nose. Then he turned to Jack and Annie. "Afraid I have to leave y'all now," Dipper said. "But it's been great."

"Yeah, um . . . ," Jack began, trying to think of a good reason to stay with Dipper.

"I'd like to hear you blow that horn when the time's right," Dipper said to Annie. "And don't forget to say hi to Teddy and Kathleen for me." He winked, then waved and started walking away.

"But—but, Dipper!" called Jack.

"Sorry, man! I'm late!" Dipper shouted over his shoulder. "Thanks a million!" He waved again and kept going.

Jack and Annie looked at each other in a panic. "We have to stay with him!" said Annie. "Wait, wait, Dipper!" She and Jack ran after him.

"Where are you going now?" Jack asked.

"My next job," said Dipper. "I have to haul bananas till dark."

"Really? *Another* job?" said Jack.

"Hey, guess what?" shouted Annie. "We *love* to haul bananas!"

"Yeah. Yeah, we do," said Jack.

Dipper stopped and stared at them. "What is wrong with y'all?" he said. "Don't you know how to have fun?"

Jack didn't know what to say.

"Seriously," said Annie. "We *do* love to haul bananas. And you make everything more fun with your singing."

"Yeah, you're a good singer!" piped up Jack. "That's a gift!"

Dipper just shook his head. "Remember when I said you didn't have any more brains than a pair of potatoes? Well, I take it back. I don't think you have *one* potato's brain between you."

Jack and Annie laughed.

"Well, come on, then," said Dipper.

Jack and Annie hurried with Dipper down to the loading dock on the riverfront. At least fifty workers were hauling huge loads of bananas out of the cargo hold of a ship.

"Wait here," Dipper told them.

Dipper walked over to a man checking people in to work. He pointed to Jack and Annie. The man shrugged, then nodded. Dipper waved for them to come join him.

Jack and Annie ran down to join Dipper and the other workers in the cargo hold. Dipper picked up a giant bunch of bananas. The bunch was almost as big as Annie! He hauled it onto his shoulder and then picked up another one.

"Grab a bunch of bananas and follow me!" Dipper said. He headed to the counter, where men in white suits were inspecting the banana bunches.

"No way either of us can pick up one of those bunches," Jack said to Annie.

"Let's try it together," said Annie.

Annie hid their trumpet behind a large wooden box. Jack put his bag there, too. Jack and Annie loaded a bunch of bananas into their arms. They walked closely together, taking short, clumsy steps, following Dipper. They delivered the bunch to the inspectors and then hurried back to get another.

As the sun sank toward the river, Jack, Annie, and Dipper hauled bananas back and forth between the cargo hold and the inspectors. They hauled bananas until it was almost dark. Jack was so tired he could hardly see straight. He was afraid Dipper would never call it quits.

"Last one," Dipper said finally.

Yes! thought Jack. They grabbed their last loads.

Suddenly a large rat jumped out of the cargo hold! Dipper let out a scream. He dropped his bananas and took off running. Annie and Jack dropped their bananas, too. Annie grabbed her trumpet. Jack grabbed his bag, and they ran after Dipper.

Running like crazy, Dipper led Jack and Annie far from the loading area—and the rat. When he finally stopped, Jack bumped into Dipper, and Annie bumped into Jack. They all started laughing. Dipper laughed the hardest. He collapsed on the curb of Decatur Street and laughed so hard his whole body shook. Jack and Annie sat down next to him, laughing until they cried. Finally they all managed to calm down.

"I know . . . I know I said I wasn't afraid of anything," Dipper said breathlessly. "But I lied. I'm afraid of one thing: rats. Rats give me the heebie-jeebies."

"Yeah, yeah," Annie said, catching her breath. "I know how you feel. Spiders give *me* the heebie-jeebies."

"Yeah," Jack said, panting. "Yeah, actually, ghosts give 'em to me."

"That's cool, that's cool, man," said Dipper. "Between the three of us, we got all the scaredy stuff covered."

That made them all start laughing again. As the twilight deepened, they sat on the curb, catching their breath. They laughed now and then, out of relief and friendship.

Then Dipper stood up. "Before we part ways, I better get our pay from the boss. Hold on."

Jack and Annie kept sitting on the curb as Dipper ran back down to the dock. "*Part ways?* We can't part ways yet," said Jack.

"I know!" said Annie. "We haven't even begun to accomplish our mission."

"Umbrella! Buy an umbrella!" a man shouted as he walked by. He carried a load of umbrellas on his back. “Storm a-comin’! Big storm comin’ for the eve of All Saints’!”

“Oh, no, now a storm’s coming,” said Jack. He was confused about what they should do next.

A moment later, Dipper returned. “Thirty cents!” he said. “We each get ten.”

“No, no, Dipper,” said Annie. “Please use it to take care of your family.”

“Yeah, do that,” said Jack.

“We insist,” said Annie.

Dipper smiled. “Oh, you do, do you? Why? What’s this game y’all are playing?”

“It’s no game,” said Jack.

“We’re just a couple of potato heads,” said Annie. “Get used to it.”

“Well, then, you two potato heads, let me give you something else,” said Dipper. “Come along with me.”

“Great!” said Jack. They weren’t “parting ways” yet! He and Annie jumped up from the curb and bounded off with Dipper.

CHAPTER SIX

Find Me at the Greasy Spoon

Streetlamps were coming on as Jack, Annie, and Dipper walked away from Jackson Square. When they came to Bourbon Street, vendors walked the sidewalks, calling out, "Ice cream!" "Lemon pie!" "Ham biscuits!"

"Hmm. Sounds good," said Annie. "There seems to be lots of good food in New Orleans."

"Best in the world!" said Dipper.

People were sitting outside dance halls and restaurants, laughing and talking, eating and drinking. Outside and inside, musicians were blaring away on their instruments.

"Hey, there's Dipper! Sing something for us, Dipper!" the ice cream lady yelled.

Dipper waved and kept going.

"Hey, girl, can you play that trumpet?" a man called to Annie.

"Not till the time's right!" Annie shouted.

"When's that?" the man said.

"She'll know it when she feels it!" Dipper shouted.

At the end of the block, under a streetlamp, a trio was singing in harmony. It was Little Mac, Happy, and Big Nose Sidney.

"Look, Dipper, it's your friends again," said Annie.

"I see 'em," said Dipper. But he ignored the three boys and crossed the street.

Dipper led Jack and Annie down a narrow alley to the back of a shabby, run-down building. Good cooking smells came from inside. "Y'all wait for me outside this greasy spoon," he said, and he slipped through the back door.

"What's a *greasy spoon*?" asked Annie.

"Smells like it must be a restaurant," said Jack.

Annie put down the trumpet. Jack put down his bag. They sat on the back steps of the greasy spoon. While they waited in the muggy twilight for Dipper, Jack wiped his forehead. He was starving and ached all over.

Soon Dipper pushed open the back door with his foot. He was carrying a big bowl and a tall glass. "I got us some gumbo stew and some lemonade to share!" he said. "Talk about good!"

"Oh, man, thanks," breathed Jack.

Dipper sat between Jack and Annie on the steps. He pulled spoons out of his pocket for each of them. "Dig in, y'all!" he said.

Together the three of them tackled the gumbo stew. They all ate their fill of spicy chicken, ham, tomatoes, okra, onions, and rice. When the bowl was empty, they shared the tall glass of lemonade. Then they sat back on the steps and heaved big sighs. Jack felt stuffed and happy.

"Mighty fine," breathed Dipper.

"Mighty fine," echoed Jack.

"*Mighty* fine," said Annie.

"Nothing tastes as good as gumbo after a hard day's work," said Dipper. He stood up. "Well, I have to leave y'all now. Thanks a million for your help today. And don't forget to thank Teddy and Kathleen for sending y'all to find me." Before Jack and Annie could stop him, Dipper climbed down the steps and vanished into the dark.

"Dipper?" called Jack.

There was no answer.

"He's gone again!" said Annie.

"And we totally failed in our mission for Merlin," said Jack. "We didn't help Dipper get on the right path to give his gifts to the world."

"I know. We have to find him. Come on," said Annie. She hopped up and headed after Dipper.

"Wait, the trumpet!" said Jack. He grabbed the magic trumpet and his bag and followed her.

When Jack left the steps, it was too dark for

him to see where Annie had gone. Thunder rumbled in the distance. The air felt heavy and thick as if the storm were about to break at any moment.

"Annie!" Jack called.

"Here!" Annie called back from the front of the restaurant. Jack joined her. Together they peeked through a window that looked into a large kitchen. Dipper was alone, washing a mountain of dishes.

"Why's he doing that?" whispered Jack.

"Hey, Dipper!" said Annie.

Dipper turned and smiled. "You caught me," he said. He looked embarrassed.

"Why are you washing dishes?" asked Annie.

Dipper shrugged. "Got to pay for our dinner somehow," he said.

"We'll help you," said Annie.

"We love washing dishes!" said Jack.

Dipper laughed. "Then come on in, potato heads," he said. "I could use some help."

Jack and Annie slipped through a side door into the hot, steamy kitchen.

Jack put down his bag and the trumpet. He and Annie picked up dirty plates from the counter. They began scraping leftovers into a garbage pail. They scraped fish heads, oyster shells, crab legs, shrimp tails, chicken bones, grease, and gravy off dozens of plates.

The work was messy and smelly. But Jack and Annie worked hard to keep up with Dipper. Every time he took a plate from them, he smiled and said, "Thank you." He never frowned or complained or even seemed tired.

"Dipper," said Annie while they worked, "your life seems really hard. How do you stay so cheerful?"

"Why not? It's more fun to be cheerful than sad," he said.

"Don't you ever feel like getting mad or complaining about stuff?" said Jack.

"Sure I do, I'm human," said Dipper. "I feel all kinds of things. All day long I feel things. You could say I have a rich life. I might not get to *have* everything. But I get to *feel* everything!" He laughed.

"I'm the same way," said Annie.

"I thought so," said Dipper. "That's why I sure would like to hear you play that trumpet sometime."

"Maybe you will," said Annie.

By the time they finished washing dishes, rain was falling outside.

"Where to now?" said Jack.

"One more treat for y'all," said Dipper. "Let's leave this greasy spoon and head back down to the river. To the River Café for dessert! Come on."

"We better not," said Jack. "The waiters there don't like us."

"Don't worry about them," said Dipper. "You're with me now."

Jack and Annie followed Dipper outside into the rain. The wind was blowing harder now. "Uh-oh," said Dipper. "Here comes the storm! Let's hurry!"

Thunder cracked and rain began to pour down. The three of them got soaked as they hurried through the alley back to Bourbon Street.

The street was empty now. Partygoers and street musicians had fled from the storm. The restaurants and cafés had taken their chairs and tables inside. Lightning lit the sky, and thunder shook the ground. The wind was blowing hard, picking up sticks and leaves and trash.

"We have to find cover!" said Dipper. "Run!" He and Jack and Annie bowed their heads against the downpour and ran up Bourbon Street.

"Dipper! Over here, man!" someone yelled. It was Little Mack.

Little Mack, Happy, and Big Nose Sidney were waving to Dipper from the doorway of a dark building on a corner. Dipper, Jack, and Annie ran across the street through the pounding rain.

"Get over here, out of the street!" shouted Little Mack. "Before you get hit by lightning!"

"Thanks, fellas!" said Dipper.

Soaking wet, Jack, Annie, Dipper, Little Mack, Happy, and Big Nose Sidney all crowded together just inside the dark building, looking out at the storm.

"Who lives here?" asked Dipper.

"Nobody. It's been empty for years," said Happy.

"Used to be a blacksmith shop," said Little Mack.

"Lafitte's Blacksmith Shop?" said Jack. He immediately stepped out of the shop and stood under the eaves.

"Yeah, what's wrong with that?" asked Little Mack.

"We read this place is haunted!" said Annie.

"Y'all believe in ghosts?" asked Little Mack.

"No, not really," said Jack.

"But I thought you said they gave you the heebie—" started Dipper.

"No, no, I was kidding," Jack said quickly. He didn't want Dipper's friends to know he was afraid of ghosts.

Lightning split the sky again. Another crash of thunder shattered the night. The wind blew so hard that shingles blew off the roof across the street and crashed to the sidewalk.

"Whoa! Come inside, man, we gotta close the door, " Dipper said to Jack.

"Hold on," said Little Mack. "We have to go."

"We do?" asked Happy.

Little Mack whispered something to Happy and Big Nose Sidney.

"Oh, yeah, he's right," said Happy. "We have to leave. We'll see y'all later."

"Y'all are scared to stay here, aren't you?" said Dipper.

"No, man. We forgot we have an important gig to play," said Big Nose Sidney.

"Oh. Suddenly y'all have got an important gig. I see. . . ," said Dipper.

"Yeah, we'll have to try to make it through the storm. See y'all! Come on, fellas!" said Little Mack.

The three boys hurried out of the blacksmith shop and turned the corner.

"They left 'cause they're scaredy-cats," said Dipper, chuckling.

"Yeah," said Jack, "scaredy-cats."

Thunder cracked the sky again, the loudest crack so far. It seemed to shake the whole block. Roof shingles flew through the air.

"Come back inside!" said Dipper. "It's dangerous out there."

Jack took a deep breath and stepped back into Lafitte's Blacksmith Shop.

CHAPTER SEVEN

Skid-Dat-De-Dat!

Dipper closed the door.

It was pitch-black inside the shop. As the wind howled outside, the broken shutters banged against the brick walls. A gust of damp air blew through the room.

"It's dark in here," said Annie. "And cold."

"It's creepy," said Jack.

"Yup," said Dipper. "Let's leave. I've changed my mind about staying here. We can find some other place to get out of the storm."

"Good idea," said Annie.

"*Great* idea!" said Jack.

Jack heard Dipper rattle the door handle. "Uh-oh," said Dipper.

"Uh-oh what?" said Jack.

"Won't open," said Dipper. "It's stuck."

Jack felt the hair rise on the back of his neck. The shutters banged in the wind.

"Hold on a second, I've got some matches in my pocket," said Dipper. "I just hope they didn't get wet in the rain."

Jack heard Dipper trying to strike a match. He tried one, two, three times—then he held up a small flame.

"Yay," breathed Annie.

Jack looked around the room. In the dancing light, he could make out wooden buckets on the floor, a couple of broken chairs, a doorway leading to a back room, and—

Squeak! A bat flapped above their heads.

"Ahhh!" Jack, Annie, and Dipper ducked.

The match went out.

Dipper quickly lit another match. He held it up high, trying to light the room. Jack didn't see the bat, but he saw a bricked-over fireplace, some rusty lanterns, and *lots* of spiderwebs.

"Yikes!" said Annie.

The match went out.

"Help," said Annie in a small voice. "More light, please."

"Nobody panic," said Dipper. "I got two matches left."

"Just two?" said Annie.

"Hey, I thought I saw some lanterns," said Jack. "Near the fireplace. Maybe we could light *them.*"

"Good idea," said Dipper. "Maybe there's oil still in 'em. I just hope I can light the wicks. Or we'll be left in the dark with the bats."

"And spiders," said Annie.

And ghosts, Jack thought.

Dipper struck his next-to-last match. He held it up to find the lanterns.

"Over here," said Jack, pointing.

"I see," said Dipper. But as he knelt on the floor, the match went out. "I got just one more," he whispered. "So we better be *real* careful."

Dipper lit his last match. Jack slowly lifted the glass on both the lanterns. Very carefully, Dipper touched the match flame to the wick of the first lantern. The wick sputtered and flickered to life. A yellow glow filled the room.

"Ahh!" said Dipper. He lit the second lantern. "Beautiful. You can each carry one."

Jack picked up one of the lanterns. Annie put down her trumpet and picked up the other one. The firelight cast eerie shadows on the walls.

Screeeee!

A sound from the back room startled them. It sounded like the creak of a door opening. Jack's heart began to pound.

WHAM! The sound of a door slamming shut!

Jack's heart beat faster and faster.

"Hey!" called Dipper. "Who's back there?"

No one answered.

Clump. Clump. Clump. The sound of footsteps on stairs!

Jack held his breath.

"Who's there?" yelled Dipper.

"WOOOOOOO!"

"Show yourself!" yelled Dipper.

The shutters outside banged harder against the walls.

"WOOOOOOO!"

"Mercy," whispered Dipper.

Jack's hand trembled, shaking the lantern and making the shadows in the room dance even more wildly.

The moaning came again: "WOOOOOOO!"

"Annie!" said Jack. "The trumpet! The time is right!"

"I know it! I feel it!" said Annie. She put down her lantern and grabbed the trumpet. "Sing, Jack!"

Annie lifted the magic trumpet to her lips and blew. A pure, smooth sound flowed from the trumpet and filled the room. As Annie played, Jack started singing:

Ghost, ghost,
Leave us alone!
Stop, stop!
Stop your moan . . . ing!

What a stupid song, Jack thought, but they were the only words that came to his mind. Then he remembered Dipper's advice: *When you can't think of words, just sing sounds. Make 'em up. Put your heart in it.*

So Jack started singing nonsense sounds. He sang with all his heart, pouring all his feelings into the sounds, telling the ghost to go:

Skid-dat-de-dat!
Skid-dat-de-dow!
Skiddle-skiddle
Daddle-daddle
Outta here NOW!

Thumping noises came from the other room, as if heavy things were falling.

"Who's there?" shouted Dipper.

Annie stopped playing.

Jack stepped back in fear, waiting for something awful to happen. Then he heard laughing and whispering.

"Hey!" shouted Dipper. He picked up Annie's lantern and headed into the other room. Jack and Annie followed.

Little Mack, Happy, and Big Nose Sidney were crawling toward the back door.

"Stop!" yelled Dipper. "What are y'all doing here?"

The three boys all talked at once: "We fell out of the attic!" "Felt like something was pushing us out!" "Yeah! Then down the stairs and toward the door!"

"Jack's *song* pushed you downstairs!" said Annie, laughing. "He ordered the ghost to leave us alone! His singing was magic."

"Your playing was magic, too!" Dipper said to Annie. "You two really put your hearts in it."

"Thanks," said Jack.

Dipper looked down at Little Mack. "Now tell us what you three fools were up to!" he said.

"We decided to play a joke on y'all," said Little Mack. "So we snuck through the back door and up to the attic."

"We thought you left because you were scared of ghosts!" said Annie.

"Heck no, man," said Little Mack.

"We're not afraid of ghosts," said Happy.

"Not even a little bit," said Big Nose Sidney.

Suddenly a cold wind blasted through the room. The lanterns flickered out. An eerie green light lit the blacksmith shop.

"WHAT?" a voice roared. *"NOT AFRAID OF GHOSTS?"*

The voice seemed to come from everywhere—and nowhere.

"AHHHHHHH!" the kids all screamed together.

"HAH-HAH-HAH!" Mean-sounding laughter echoed through the shop. It grew louder and louder. "HAH-HAH-HAH!"

"AHHHHHHH!" the kids all screamed again.

Stomping noises thundered in the attic overhead.

Everyone shrieked and froze with terror.

Down from the attic came a pirate. His face

was hidden by the brim of a black hat. He wore a gray jacket with a double row of buttons, a red sash, and dark pants tucked inside black boots.

The pirate looked like a real person, *except you could see right through him.*

CHAPTER EIGHT

Heebie Jeebies

Thunder shook the night. The wind howled. The pirate ghost floated down the stairs.

"The ghost of Jean Lafitte!" whispered Annie.

The ghost pointed a bony finger at Happy. "NOT AFRAID OF GHOSTS?" his voice boomed again. He pointed at Big Nose Sidney. "NOT EVEN A LITTLE BIT? HAH-HAH-HAH!"

"AHHHHHHH!" everyone shrieked again. They all scrambled out of the back room to the front room. They pushed on the front door together. But the door still wouldn't open.

"SCURVY DOGS! YOU CANNOT ESCAPE ME!" the ghost of Jean Lafitte shouted.

The pirate ghost floated to the center of the room and stopped. He rested his hands on his hips, threw back his head, and laughed again. "YOU'RE TRAPPED NOW!" Jean Lafitte roared. "TRAPPED HERE FOREVER!"

To Jack's horror, more ghost pirates began gliding through the walls into the room. One at a time they came: a pirate with a gold earring, another with a pistol, one with a head scarf, another with an eye patch, one with a saber, another with a bushy beard, one with a thin mustache, another with a sack, one with a striped shirt, another with a peg leg.

Finally ten ghost pirates circled the room!

From the center of the circle, Jean Lafitte let out another peal of mean laughter. "HAH-HAH-HAH!"

The pirate crew snorted, snarled, and growled, "YARRR! ARGHH! ARRL!"

Suddenly Jack started singing:

Skiddle-diddle dog!
Hey, hey, hey!
Ghost, go away,
Go away, go away!

"Jack!" said Annie. "What are you doing?"

"Play, Annie! Play!" squeaked Jack.

"I can't!" said Annie. "We used up the magic! It's just an ordinary trumpet now!"

"Here, give it to me!" said Dipper.

Annie handed Dipper the trumpet.

Dipper put the trumpet to his lips. He closed his eyes. He took a deep breath, and then he blew. The air vibrated with a single warm note. Then Dipper's fingers danced over the trumpet's valves. A lively, swinging tune filled the blacksmith shop.

Jean Lafitte stopped laughing his mean laugh. He held up his hands for his crew to be silent. As Dipper played, crooked smiles crossed the pirates' faces.

Dipper's joyful music drowned out the noise of the storm outside. Annie snatched two rungs from a broken chair. She used them as drumsticks, tapping them against a wooden bucket. Jack grabbed two more rungs and did the same.

Dipper paused long enough to yell to his trio, "Hey, boys! Sing the Heebie-Jeebie song!"

"We don't know it!" said Little Mack.

"Make somethin' up!" called Dipper.

As Dipper played the trumpet, Little Mack sang:

I got the heebies!
You got the jeebies!

Then Happy sang:

The heebies make you hop!
And the jeebies make you quake!

Then Big Nose Sidney sang:

Do a little dance, Mama!
Stomp and shake!

As the trio sang, the ghost of Jean Lafitte started to dance. He shook his head and clapped his hands. He waved his arms through the air. He turned in a circle. "Go, Mama, go!" he shouted.

Lafitte's crew began dancing like their captain. All the ghost pirates moved in a circle, shaking their heads and waving their hands. Some floated off the floor, turning this way and that.

Little Mack sang:

Hey, Papa! Hey, Mama!
Hey! Hey! Hey!

"Hey, hey, hey!" all the pirates shouted. "Hey, hey, hey!"

Dipper played the trumpet. Jack and Annie drummed on the bucket. The trio sang. The floor shook. The windows rattled. And all the pirates stomped and shook, doing the Heebie-Jeebie dance.

"SWING THAT MUSIC!" shouted Jean Lafitte's ghost.

"YARR!" the pirates all shouted. "YARR! YARR!"

The front door suddenly banged open.

"GO, MAMA! GO, PAPA! GO! GO! GO!" shouted the ghost of Jean Lafitte. He danced out of the shop, and his pirate crew followed, one by one.

As the ghosts all danced out of the shop, Dipper kept playing. The trio kept singing, and Jack and Annie kept drumming.

"MY CREW AND I SURE ENJOYED YOUR VISIT!" the pirate ghost captain shouted back to Dipper and the others. "BE SURE TO COME BACK! SAME TIME NEXT YEAR!"

The ghost of Jean Lafitte turned and waved his arms in the air again. "COME ON, BOYS! PAPA'S DOIN' THE HEEBIE-JEEBIES DANCE!" Then, doing the Heebie-Jeebies dance, *all* the pirate ghosts danced away into the dark New Orleans night.

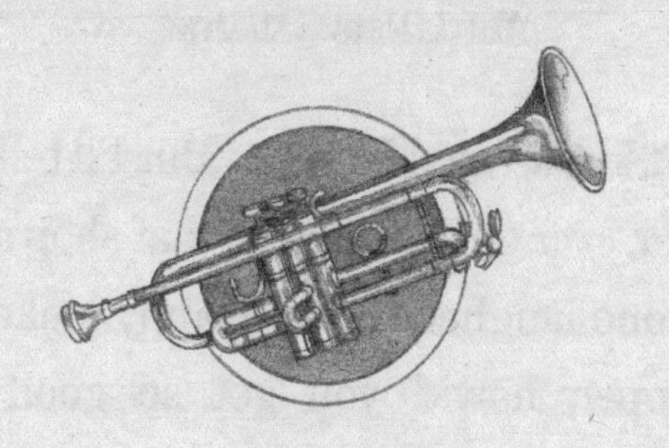

CHAPTER NINE

Working Man Blues

Dipper stopped playing. The three boys stopped singing. Jack and Annie stopped drumming.

There was silence. They all crept to the open doorway and stepped outside. The rain had stopped, and the wind had died down. The air felt clean and cool. Stars shone overhead. The pirate ghosts were gone.

"Whoa, that was something!" said Little Mack. "What just happened?"

"Was it a dream?" asked Big Nose Sidney. "Were those ghosts real?"

"I don't know," said Dipper. "But I'll tell you this: you'll never, *ever* get me back in that shop again."

Everyone laughed. Even Happy looked happy. "Hey, Dipper, how'd you get so good on that horn?" he asked, grinning.

"I practiced for two years at the Waif's Home," said Dipper. "That's how."

"You got to blow that horn while we sing!" said Big Nose Sidney. "Come with us now! We really do have an important gig tonight on a riverboat!"

"A riverboat?" Jack and Annie said together. They looked at each other. Their research book said that Louis Armstrong developed his musical talents performing on riverboats!

"That's right," said Little Mack.

"Oh, wow, Dipper, you have to go with them!" said Annie.

"Yeah, man!" said Jack.

But Dipper just shook his head. "Sorry, folks, but I can't play tonight. I have to get up early in the morning to haul coal."

"Aww, Dipper," said Little Mack.

"Aww, Dipper," said Jack.

"Don't y'all worry about me," said Dipper. "Have a good time on the boat, fellas. Hang on to that smile, Happy."

"I'll try," said Happy.

"See you later," said Big Nose Sidney.

"So long to y'all, too," Little Mack said to Jack and Annie.

"Bye," said Jack.

"Good luck on your gig," said Annie. The three boys waved and took off.

Dipper looked after them for a long moment. Then he turned to Jack and Annie.

"Here's your horn back," he said. "Thanks for letting me play it." He handed the trumpet to Annie.

"Do you want to keep it?" she said.

"No, thanks. I have my own horn back at my house, a cornet they gave me at the Waif's Home," said Dipper. "Someday when I'm grown, maybe I'll bring it out again."

"I think you should have gone with the fellas,

Dipper," said Jack, "to share your musical gifts—"

"I know, I know," said Dipper, "to share my musical gifts with the world." He shook his head as if he were shaking off the thought. Then he beamed a big smile at Jack and Annie. "Hey! Weren't we talking about dessert a little while back? That's a gig I can get behind and still get some sleep. Come on!"

As Dipper led Jack and Annie down the rain-slicked street, the wet sidewalks glistened like silver. Life had returned to the French Quarter. Horses and mules splashed through puddles. Streetlamps burned brightly outside dance halls and restaurants. Waiters carried tables and chairs back outside.

When Dipper, Jack, and Annie came to Jackson Square, they found kids playing music again. A band was playing a song Jack knew: "When the Saints Go Marching In." A few people in costumes were wandering about.

Dipper led Jack and Annie to the back door of

the River Café. "The cook here is a friend of mine. So don't worry about the waiters," he said with a wink. "Be back in a minute." He slipped into the café kitchen.

As Jack and Annie waited for Dipper, they could hear the jazzy music coming from the square:

Oh, when the saints go marching in,
Oh, when the saints go marching in.

"Teddy was right. I love New Orleans," said Annie.

"Me too," said Jack. "But how are we ever going to accomplish our mission for Merlin? Dipper seems like he's never going to change his mind about making music."

"I know," said Annie. "In fact, I was just thinking that we might have to do something really drastic."

"What's that?" said Jack.

"Show him our research book," said Annie.

"Whoa!" said Jack. "Do you really think—"

Before Jack could finish, Dipper came back outside. "Mmm-mmm! Talk about something good!" he said. He clutched a greasy napkin filled with freshly made doughnuts. "Follow me."

As Jack and Annie followed Dipper to the river, Jack's mind was racing. *Should* they show Dipper the research book? It would prove they'd come from the future. What would Dipper say? What would he think? *It's too weird,* Jack thought.

"Let's just try talking to him first," Jack whispered to Annie. She nodded.

Dipper led them to a bench near the water. Jack and Annie sat on the wet wood on either side of him. Dipper unwrapped the doughnuts and handed one to Jack and one to Annie and kept one for himself.

"Careful," Dipper said. "The sugar will get all over y'all."

Jack lifted the warm, sticky doughnut to his mouth and took a big bite. Powdered sugar, flour, butter, vanilla—all melted in his mouth. It was mighty good.

Nobody talked while they ate their doughnuts. When they were finished, they all wiped their sticky fingers on their shirts and pants. By now, Jack's clothes were soaked with rainwater, coal dust, kitchen grease, sweat, and grime. *A little powdered sugar and butter won't make a bit of difference*, he thought.

"So, Dipper," said Annie. "You know you're a really great musician, don't you?"

Dipper smiled at her.

"Actually, you're a creative genius," added Jack.

Dipper laughed out loud. "And y'all know who *you* are, don't you?"

"Yup, the biggest potato heads you ever met," finished Jack.

"But *this* time we're *right*," said Annie.

"Nope, sorry," said Dipper. "I'm definitely no genius. The truth is I never got past elementary school. I don't even know how to read music."

"But don't you love to *play* music?" said Annie.

"Yeah, sure, I do. Somehow I've got music in my bones," said Dipper. "Sad to say, *all* I really ever want to do is blow my horn."

"Then why don't you?" said Jack. He felt desperate. Even without their mission for Merlin, it seemed incredibly sad that Dipper had turned his back on his music.

"Yeah, why don't you go play on the riverboat with the fellas?" said Annie. "It wouldn't hurt you to miss a few hours' sleep."

Dipper took a deep breath and let it out slowly. "When I was twelve years old, I got too rowdy one time," he said. "It was New Year's Eve. I was singing with the fellas, and I got carried away and fired off a gun . . . just into the air. I wasn't trying to hurt anybody. But I got caught and I got sentenced to two years in the Waif's Home. I just got out a little while ago. I feel really bad for letting my family down like that. So right now, all I want to do is help them by keeping a steady job."

"But what about a job playing music?" said Jack. "Great musicians can make a lot of money and help their families."

"Not playing the music *I* want to play," said Dipper. "At least I haven't met any. Have you?"

"Yes. Actually, we have," said Annie. She turned and looked at Jack. "We have to do it."

Jack sighed, then nodded slowly. Annie was right. He reached into his bag and pulled out their research book.

CHAPTER TEN

Thanks a Million

Jack pushed his glasses into place and opened *A History of New Orleans Music.*

"What's that, man?" Dipper asked.

"It's a history book," said Jack.

"Teddy and Kathleen gave it to us," said Annie.

"Oh, yeah, my best friends," said Dipper.

Jack looked in the index of the book. He found the right page and turned to it.

"I'm going to read something to you, man," said Jack. "Just listen." And Jack read:

As a young teenager, Louis Armstrong

> **often performed with "kid bands" on the streets of the city. Eventually he played with older musicians in dance halls, and he developed his musical talents performing on Mississippi riverboats. When he was twenty-one, he moved to Chicago, where he played in the well-known band of his old friend Joe Oliver.**

"Joe Oliver?" said Dipper. "Joe's in that book? *I'm* in that book?"

"Yep. Hold on, there's more," said Jack. He read:

> **Over time, Louis Armstrong became world-famous, but he always called New Orleans home. The city honored him by naming a large park the Louis Armstrong Park. It also named its airport the Louis Armstrong International Airport.**

"What's that? *International airport?*" asked Dipper.

"That's where planes fly in and out from all over the world," said Annie.

Dipper started laughing. "Y'all are pulling my leg."

"No," said Jack. "We're not. Look at *this*, Dipper." He held up the book and showed Dipper the picture of Louis Armstrong, the King of Jazz, playing the trumpet in front of a huge crowd. "That's you, Dipper."

Jack waited for Dipper to laugh and say the picture wasn't him. But Dipper stopped smiling and nodded. "Yeah. Yeah, I've seen that picture before," he said softly.

"You *have*?" said Jack, stunned.

"You've seen *this* picture before?" said Annie. "Where?"

"Here." Dipper touched his chest. "Here, in my heart. It's the picture I've had in my heart for a long time, like a dream. Hey, y'all, is this a dream?"

Jack and Annie laughed. Annie smiled. "Yes, you could say that," she said.

"But it's a *true* dream," said Jack.

"Keep that picture in your heart, Dipper," said Annie. "Hold it close to you, and one day you'll be living it. We promise."

For a long time the three of them just stared at the picture. When Jack looked at Dipper again, he saw tears glisten in Dipper's eyes.

"Okay, I'll do that," said Dipper. He wiped his eyes with the palms of his hands. "I think I can keep my jobs and start making a little room for my music, too."

"Yes!" said Annie.

"Maybe you should go play with the fellas on the riverboat tonight," said Jack.

"Yeah, maybe I'll try and do that," said Dipper.

"Great!" said Annie.

Jack heaved a sigh and put away their book.

Dipper stood up. "But now y'all have to get going. On the eve of All Saints' Day, there's a curfew for kids under thirteen. They have to be off the streets by nine, or the paddy wagon will pick 'em up."

"So . . . you're definitely on the path to sharing your musical gift with the world. Right, man?" asked Jack.

Dipper laughed. "I reckon I am," he said. "Thanks to a couple of potato heads."

"Okay, good," said Jack. He and Annie stood up. "To get home, we need to walk to Bourbon Street and catch a streetcar to Canal Street."

"Let's go," said Dipper.

The three of them left the waterfront. They walked past Jackson Square and headed past the cathedral on St. Peter Street.

"I'll walk y'all back to Bourbon Street," said Dipper.

"Then do you have time to ride back with us to Canal Street?" said Annie. "So we can hang out together a little longer on the train?"

"You know I can't do that," said Dipper. "They won't let me sit with y'all on the streetcar."

"Why not?" asked Jack.

"I'd have to sit in the back while y'all sit up front," said Dipper.

"What are you talking about?" said Annie.

"Y'all are white. I'm black," said Dipper.

"So?" said Annie.

"Black folks aren't allowed to sit with white folks. That's the way it is," said Dipper.

"Are you kidding? That's crazy!" said Annie.

"No, I'm not kidding," said Dipper. He stopped walking and looked closely at Jack and Annie. "Where are y'all from? How'd you get that crazy history book with my picture in it? And why did y'all come here to find me?"

"It's really, really hard to explain, Dipper," said Jack. "But just know this: one day things are going to change. *Everybody* will sit together on trains and buses and planes."

"And one day an African American man will run for president of the United States," said Annie. "And millions of people—of all colors—will vote for him."

"And he'll win!" said Jack.

Dipper laughed and shook his head. “Okay, now I know I’m dreaming,” he said, “but I really like this dream.”

“It’s the truth,” said Annie. “We promise.”

By now they had come to the corner of St. Peter and Bourbon Street. “This is where I leave you,” said Dipper.

Annie threw her arms around Dipper and gave him a big hug. “Good-bye, Dipper!”

Jack did the same. “Bye, man,” he said. “Thanks a million.”

“Same to you,” said Dipper. “Hey, there’s your streetcar now.”

The streetcar glided to a stop at the corner. Jack and Annie hopped aboard and sat in front. As the streetcar went up Bourbon Street, they stuck their heads out the window and waved to Dipper. He waved back. Jack and Annie waved and waved, until they couldn’t see Dipper anymore.

CHAPTER ELEVEN

Swing that Music

As the streetcar rumbled down Canal Street, Jack looked over his shoulder. Dipper was right. African Americans were sitting in the back, while only white people were in the front. Jack hadn't even noticed it on their first streetcar ride.

Jack's heart felt heavy. *Why would anyone not want to sit next to someone just because they are a different color?* he wondered. *How could anyone ever be mean to Dipper? Dipper, who is gentle and friendly and kind? Dipper, who hears music everywhere?*

Jack listened to the *click-clack* of the streetcar rolling down the tracks. The sound had a good beat. Jack tapped his hand against his knee, until the streetcar came to a stop.

"Let's go," said Annie.

Jack and Annie stood up. Canal Street was bright with lights. People were still selling things on the sidewalk.

"What time is it, please?" Jack asked the conductor.

"Five minutes after nine, boy," said the conductor. "Y'all better head for home."

"We are!" said Annie.

Jack and Annie hopped off the streetcar and started to run. They ran to the bottom of Canal Street and crossed to the palm trees in the grove near the Mississippi River. In the dark, they found the rope ladder and scrambled up it into the tree house.

Jack grabbed the Pennsylvania book that would take them home.

"Wait!" said Annie, looking out the window. "Look!"

A brightly lit Mississippi showboat was rolling up the river. A large paddle wheel behind the boat was

churning the water. Music was coming from on board.

Annie grabbed Jack's arm. "Listen! The 'Heebie-Jeebies'!" she said.

Jack listened. He could hear the trio singing: Little Mack, Happy, and Big Nose Sidney. But the best sound of all was the bright sound of a horn sailing through the New Orleans night.

"It's Dipper!" said Annie. "It's got to be!"

"He caught the boat!" said Jack. "Just in time!"

Jack and Annie listened to the joyful swinging sound of Dipper's music until the riverboat rolled out of sight.

Jack heaved a happy sigh. Then he pointed at their Pennsylvania book. "I wish we could go home," he said.

The wind began to blow.

The tree house started to spin.

It spun faster and faster.

Then everything was still.

Absolutely still.

♪ ♪ ♪

Jack and Annie were wearing their own clothes again. Rain tapped gently against the roof of the tree house. A cool breeze blew through the window.

"We have to get home before Mom and Dad wake up," said Annie.

"Right," said Jack. He pulled *A History of New Orleans Music* out of his backpack and left it on the floor.

Annie put the trumpet beside it. Then they headed down the rope ladder. They pulled up their rain hoods. As they tramped in their boots through the wet autumn woods, they were both quiet.

Finally Annie said, "I feel good."

"I feel good, too," said Jack. "We accomplished our mission."

"But I feel other things, too," said Annie. "I feel mad that Dipper couldn't sit on the streetcar with us."

"Me too," said Jack. "And it wasn't just in New

Orleans. A long time ago, they had laws like that in lots of places."

"Unbelievable," said Annie.

"Yeah," said Jack.

"And I feel scared when I think of those spiders in their webs," said Annie.

"Oh, they didn't bother anybody," said Jack. "But I still feel scared when I think of ghosts."

"Actually, they didn't bother anybody, either," said Annie.

"True," said Jack. "And neither did that bat."

Annie laughed. "That's true, too," she said. "I feel sad when I think we'll never see Dipper again."

"We can listen to his music," said Jack.

"Yeah . . . and I guess the music all around us will always make us think of him," said Annie. "Like right now Dipper would hear the music of the rain."

"*Tappity-tap-tap*," said Jack.

"And the music of our feet scrunching over the dead leaves—" said Annie.

"*Scrunchity-scrunch-scrunch,*" said Jack.

"*Patti-pat-pat!*" sang Annie.

"*Skid-dat-de-dat!*" sang Jack.

"*Skid-dat-de-doh!*" sang Annie.

"Go, Mama! Go!" shouted Jack.

And the two of them ran out of the Frog Creek woods and up their street, heading for home.

More Facts from Jack and Annie

• The city of New Orleans is nestled on the Mississippi River in southern Louisiana. The historic city is a blend of many cultures. Its architecture, food, and music were greatly influenced by a mix of French, Spanish, African, German, and Irish settlers.

• In 2005, New Orleans was hit by Hurricane Katrina, one of the deadliest storms in American history. Much of the city became flooded, and over 1,000 people lost their lives. The city is still rebuilding after the devastating storm.

• New Orleans is famous for being the birthplace

of jazz music. Jazz bands play in clubs and march frequently in street parades.

• The most famous parade of the year happens on Mardi Gras in late winter. On this day many thousands of tourists and townspeople participate in parties and processions.

• Louis Armstrong was born in New Orleans, Louisiana, in August 1901 and died in Queens, New York, in July 1971.

• His friends and family called him Dipper because he had a fondness as a child for a song called "Dippermouth Blues."

• All the chapter titles in this book are the titles of songs Louis Armstrong recorded early in his career.

• A year before he died, Armstrong told a reporter, "I think I had a beautiful life. I didn't wish for anything that I couldn't get and I got pretty near everything I wanted because I worked for it."*

*Quoted in *Louis Armstrong: An Extravagant Life* by Laurence Bergreen.

• In Louis Armstrong's *New York Times* obituary published on July 18, 1971, his friend and fellow musician Dizzy Gillespie wrote: "Louis is not dead, for his music is and will remain in the hearts and minds of countless millions of the world's peoples, and in the playing of hundreds of thousands of musicians who have come under his influence. The King is dead. Long live the King."

Turn the page for great activities!

Fun Activities for Jack and Annie and *You!*

Spooky Salt-Dough Ghosts

In *A Good Night for Ghosts*, Jack and Annie travel to New Orleans and run into a horde of pirate ghosts. Using your imagination and following these instructions for making salt dough, create your own horde of ghosts!

You will need:

- 1 cup flour
- 1 cup salt
- ½ cup water
- Large bowl
- Wooden spoon
- Wax paper
- Toothpicks
- Microwave-safe plate
- Permanent markers

1. Mix the flour, salt, and water in a large bowl with a wooden spoon.
2. Separate the dough into six pieces on wax paper. Some pieces can be bigger or smaller than the others to make bigger or smaller ghosts.

3. Roll each piece into a small, fat cylinder with your hands. Mold each tube into the shape of a ghost, making the head slightly smaller than the body and flattening out the bottom of the tube so that it can stand up.

4. Make small dents in the dough using a toothpick to give the ghosts eyes and mouths.

5. Have an adult help you microwave one or two ghosts at a time on the plate, checking every twenty seconds for about two minutes, until dough is firm. Your ghosts should be lying down.

6. Take the ghosts out of the microwave, but be careful—the ghosts will be hot! Let them cool, then use the markers to fill in the dents you made for the eyes and mouths.

7. Decorate the ghosts as you like! You might even want to have an adult help you superglue a magnet to the ghosts' backs and put them on the refrigerator.

Puzzle of New Orleans

Jack and Annie learned many new things on their adventure with Dipper in New Orleans. Did you?

Put your knowledge to the test! You can use a notebook or make a copy of this page if you don't want to write in your book.

1. Jack and Annie find Dipper in the __________ Quarter.

□ □ □ □ □ ○

2. What animal gives Dipper the "heebie-jeebies"?

□ ○ □

3. Jean Lafitte haunts this type of shop.

□ □ □ □ □ □ ○ □ □ □

4. What stew do Jack, Annie, and Dipper eat outside of the Greasy Spoon?

□ □ □ □ ○

5._____-singing is a type of singing that uses sounds instead of words.

6. New Orleans is a city in this state.

7. Teddy and Kathleen give this magical instrument to Annie.

Now look at your answers above. The letters that are circled complete the following sentence—but those letters are scrambled! Can you unscramble them to fill in the blanks?

Dipper was one of Louis Armstrong's famous nicknames. He was also known by the nickname _ _ _ _ _ _ _.

Answers: 1. French. 2. Rat. 3. Blacksmith. 4. Gumbo. 5. Scat. 6. Louisiana. 7. Trumpet. Final Answer: Satchmo.

Here's a special preview of

Magic Tree House® Fact Tracker

Ghosts

Help Jack and Annie track down facts about ghost stories!

Available now!

Not only does New Orleans have the most haunted bar, it also has the most haunted restaurants and the most haunted houses and theaters. No wonder people call it the most haunted city in America!

Jack and Annie's Guide to Ghost Hunting

Did you know there are people who make their living hunting ghosts? Sometimes strange things happen in a house. Objects appear to move around by themselves and noises and strange sights keep the owners awake at night. If people get really worried, they can call in professional ghost hunters to try to solve their problems.

The investigators bring their tools with them. There are thermometers to see if the air gets cold in different parts of the rooms. They also bring all kinds of cameras to catch any ghostly images that might appear and tape recorders to capture ghostly sounds.

The ghost hunters usually measure the distance between objects in a room to see if they change position. Then they take out their notebooks and record their research. Before they leave, they offer suggestions to the owners or maybe just assure them that there is nothing to worry about at all.

Does this sound like someone else we know?

The Ghost Cat of the Capitol Building

The Capitol Building is at the top of Capitol Hill near the White House. It is where the nation's lawmakers do much of their work. During the day, it's as busy as a beehive.

Workers say that at night, when all is quiet, things can get exciting down in the basement. At one time, they kept cats there to get rid of rats. Today there are no cats except for one . . . the famous ghost cat of the Capitol Building.

Some say a terrible cat haunts the basement's halls and tunnels. They say that at first the cat is the size of a kitten. But as it creeps closer, it grows *really* big . . . as big as a tiger! Its eyes burn like coals; its purr becomes a fierce growl. Legend has it that seeing the cat means that something bad is about to happen. (Yeah, like maybe a heart attack!)

The National Theatre's Friendly Ghost

For more than one hundred years, a friendly ghost is said to have haunted the National Theatre. It is supposed to be the ghost of a popular actor named John McCullough, who died in the 1800s. John was killed in a fight with another actor. His body was buried beneath the dirt floor in the cellar. Workers recently found a rusty pistol under the basement floor, but so far, no one has found any remains.

Some say that John's ghost checks the scenery and the props to make sure everything is all right. One actor even swore he saw John sitting in the audience.

The most dramatic sighting was by John's fellow actor in the late 1800s. He claimed that John's ghost appeared onstage. When the actor called out his name, the ghost quietly left.

No one is sure where John McCullough is really buried. But if you work at the National Theatre, it's nice to think John is helping you out. And you don't even have to pay him!

Enough cool facts to fill a tree house!

Jack and Annie have been all over the world in their adventures in the magic tree house. And they've learned lots of incredible facts along the way. Now they want to share them with you! Get ready for a collection of the weirdest, grossest, funniest, most all-around amazing facts that Jack and Annie have ever encountered. It's the ultimate fact attack!

Magic Tree House®

#1: Dinosaurs Before Dark
#2: The Knight at Dawn
#3: Mummies in the Morning
#4: Pirates Past Noon
#5: Night of the Ninjas
#6: Afternoon on the Amazon
#7: Sunset of the Sabertooth
#8: Midnight on the Moon
#9: Dolphins at Daybreak
#10: Ghost Town at Sundown
#11: Lions at Lunchtime
#12: Polar Bears Past Bedtime
#13: Vacation Under the Volcano
#14: Day of the Dragon King
#15: Viking Ships at Sunrise
#16: Hour of the Olympics
#17: Tonight on the *Titanic*
#18: Buffalo Before Breakfast
#19: Tigers at Twilight
#20: Dingoes at Dinnertime
#21: Civil War on Sunday
#22: Revolutionary War on Wednesday
#23: Twister on Tuesday
#24: Earthquake in the Early Morning
#25: Stage Fright on a Summer Night
#26: Good Morning, Gorillas
#27: Thanksgiving on Thursday
#28: High Tide in Hawaii

Magic Tree House® Merlin Missions

#1: Christmas in Camelot
#2: Haunted Castle on Hallows Eve
#3: Summer of the Sea Serpent
#4: Winter of the Ice Wizard
#5: Carnival at Candlelight
#6: Season of the Sandstorms
#7: Night of the New Magicians
#8: Blizzard of the Blue Moon
#9: Dragon of the Red Dawn
#10: Monday with a Mad Genius
#11: Dark Day in the Deep Sea
#12: Eve of the Emperor Penguin
#13: Moonlight on the Magic Flute
#14: A Good Night for Ghosts
#15: Leprechaun in Late Winter
#16: A Ghost Tale for Christmas Time
#17: A Crazy Day with Cobras
#18: Dogs in the Dead of Night
#19: Abe Lincoln at Last!
#20: A Perfect Time for Pandas
#21: Stallion by Starlight
#22: Hurry Up, Houdini!
#23: High Time for Heroes
#24: Soccer on Sunday
#25: Shadow of the Shark
#26: Balto of the Blue Dawn
#27: Night of the Ninth Dragon

Magic Tree House® Super Edition

#1: World at War, 1944

Magic Tree House® Fact Trackers

Dinosaurs
Knights and Castles
Mummies and Pyramids
Pirates
Rain Forests
Space
Titanic
Twisters and Other Terrible Storms
Dolphins and Sharks
Ancient Greece and the Olympics
American Revolution
Sabertooths and the Ice Age
Pilgrims
Ancient Rome and Pompeii
Tsunamis and Other Natural Disasters
Polar Bears and the Arctic
Sea Monsters
Penguins and Antarctica
Leonardo da Vinci
Ghosts
Leprechauns and Irish Folklore
Rags and Riches: Kids in the Time of Charles Dickens
Snakes and Other Reptiles
Dog Heroes
Abraham Lincoln
Pandas and Other Endangered Species
Horse Heroes
Heroes for All Times
Soccer
Ninjas and Samurai
China: Land of the Emperor's Great Wall
Sharks and Other Predators
Vikings
Dogsledding and Extreme Sports
Dragons and Mythical Creatures
World War II

More Magic Tree House®

Games and Puzzles from the Tree House
Magic Tricks from the Tree House
My Magic Tree House Journal
Magic Tree House Survival Guide
Animal Games and Puzzles
Magic Tree House Incredible Fact Book

MARY POPE OSBORNE
MAGIC
TREE HOUSE